Freshwater Lakes

Maddie Spalding

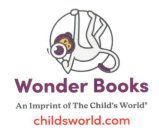

Wonder Books
An Imprint of The Child's World®
childsworld.com

Published by The Child's World®
800-599-READ • childsworld.com

Copyright © 2023 by The Child's World®
All Rights reserved. No part of this book may be reproduced or utilized in any form of by any means without written permission from the publisher.

Photography Credits
Photographs ©: Shutterstock Images, cover (trout), 1, 3 (trout), 4, 4–5, 19 (heron), 19 (beaver), 19 (fish), 19 (plants), back cover; Fernando Cristovao/Shutterstock Images, cover (background), 3 (background); Wulan Rohmawati/Shutterstock Images, 2, 14–15; Foto Request/Shutterstock Images, 6, 7, 12; iStockphoto, 8; Ronnie Howard/Shutterstock Images, 11; Rudmer Zwerver/Shutterstock Images, 16; Bambang Prihnawan/Shutterstock Images, 19 (snapping turtle); Dmytro Flisak/Shutterstock Images, 20, 21; Red Line Editorial, 22

ISBN Information
9781503858022 (Reinforced Library Binding)
9781503860322 (Portable Document Format)
9781503861688 (Online Multi-user eBook)
9781503863040 (Electronic Publication)

LCCN 2021952374

Printed in the United States of America

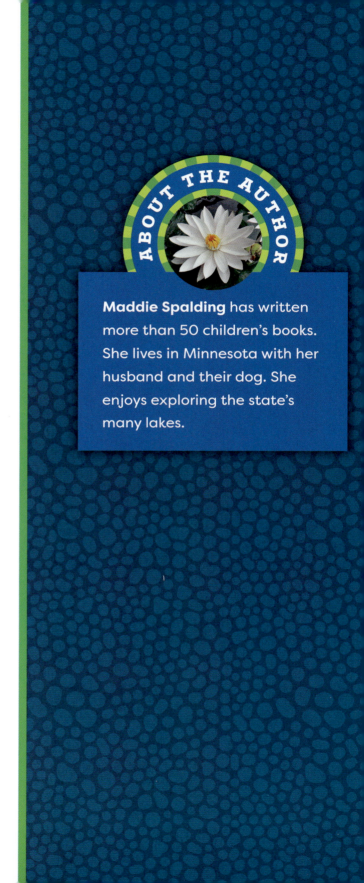

Maddie Spalding has written more than 50 children's books. She lives in Minnesota with her husband and their dog. She enjoys exploring the state's many lakes.

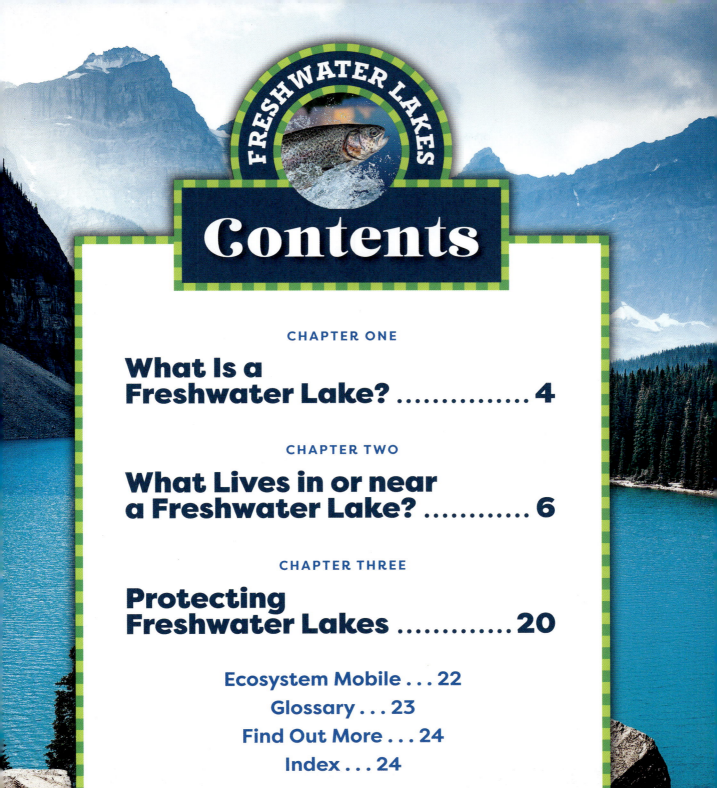

FRESHWATER LAKES

Contents

CHAPTER ONE
What Is a Freshwater Lake? 4

CHAPTER TWO
What Lives in or near a Freshwater Lake? 6

CHAPTER THREE
Protecting Freshwater Lakes 20

Ecosystem Mobile . . . 22
Glossary . . . 23
Find Out More . . . 24
Index . . . 24

CHAPTER ONE

What Is a Freshwater Lake?

On a warm summer evening, dragonflies dart above a freshwater lake. A great blue heron wades in the shallow water by the shore. It steps around water lilies. It searches for fish. The heron plunges its beak into the water. It emerges with a small fish wriggling in its beak.

This freshwater lake is full of life. Animals, plants, and insects rely on the lake to survive. They are part of an **ecosystem**. Lakes are large bodies of water surrounded by land. Most lakes are freshwater lakes. Unlike ocean water, the water in these lakes is not salty. More than 100,000 **species** of plants and animals live in freshwater ecosystems. They need fresh water to survive.

There are millions of lakes on Earth. Canada has the most lakes of any country.

Only three percent of the world's water is fresh water. The rest is salt water.

DID YOU KNOW?

CHAPTER TWO

What Lives in or near a Freshwater Lake?

GREAT BLUE HERONS

Great blue herons are large birds with blue and gray feathers. They have long legs. This helps them move through shallow waters as they hunt. The birds' necks are also long. They stretch out their necks to reach underwater **prey**. A heron's bill is sharp. The birds use their bills to spear prey. They tilt their heads back to swallow food. Great blue herons mostly eat fish and insects. They also eat animals such as frogs and snakes.

Great blue herons build nests in tall trees near water. They live in large groups. This helps protect them from **predators**. Eagles, bears, and raccoons are some animals that hunt herons. Great blue herons play an important role in the freshwater ecosystem. They control insect and fish populations. Also, some animals rely on herons as a source of food.

Herons stand very still while hunting. When prey swims by, the herons snap it up quickly.

Lake trout live in Canada and parts of the northern United States.

LAKE TROUT

Lake trout are large, gray fish with white spots. They live in freshwater streams. They also live in deep, cold areas in freshwater lakes. It is hard for predators to find these fish. The lake trout's large size makes it difficult to hunt as well. Eagles, grizzly bears, and otters are some animals that hunt lake trout.

Like great blue herons, lake trout help control insect and fish populations. Lake trout mostly eat insects and smaller fish. Many people also fish for and eat lake trout. The lake trout population went down during the 1950s. Humans fished too many lake trout during these years. Since then, people have tried to protect lake trout and increase their population. People have realized that these fish play an important role in the freshwater ecosystem.

BEAVERS

Beavers live in freshwater lakes, rivers, and swamps. They have two layers of thick, brown fur. Their outer layer of fur is waterproof. Their inner layer of fur helps keep them warm.

Beavers have webbed feet that help them swim. They also have long, flat tails. They use their tails to steer while swimming. Beavers can stay under water for up to 15 minutes at a time. They eat tree bark and water plants.

Beavers build their homes in shallow waters. These homes are called lodges. They build dams to protect their lodges. Beavers have sharp teeth that can cut tree branches. They make their dams out of mud and tree branches. Dams help freshwater ecosystems. They slow the flow of water. Dams can also block the water. This causes the water to overflow, creating a new water source where many plant and animal species can live.

DID YOU KNOW?

Beavers have special eyelids that help them see under water.

If a beaver's dam is flooded by high waters, the beaver will continue to add more wood on top.

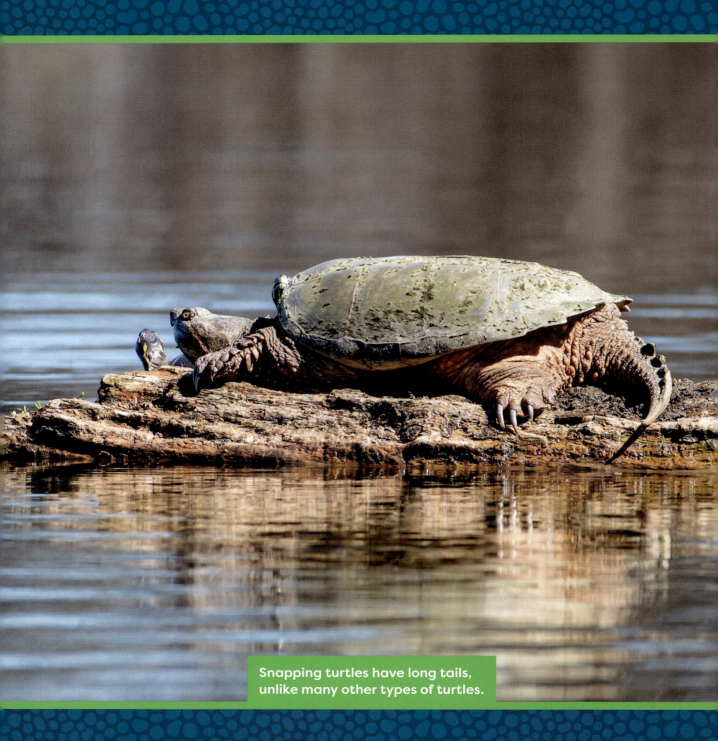

Snapping turtles have long tails, unlike many other types of turtles.

SNAPPING TURTLES

Snapping turtles are large predators. They live in freshwater lakes, ponds, and rivers. They hunt by burying themselves in mud. Their shells are brown. This helps them blend into the mud and hide. When they see prey such as fish, they strike. They extend their necks quickly. Then they bite down on prey. A snapping turtle's mouth is pointy like a beak. Snapping turtles do not have any teeth, but their bite is strong.

Snapping turtles are an important part of the freshwater lake food web. They eat fish, water plants, birds, and insects. Great blue herons and other animals eat snapping turtle eggs.

DID YOU KNOW?
The snapping turtle cannot fit inside its shell, so it uses its bite to defend itself.

WATER LILIES

Water lilies are plants in freshwater ponds and lakes. They grow in shallow waters. They usually cannot grow in water that is more than 6 feet (2 m) deep. Their dark-green leaves are round or heart shaped. These leaves are called lily pads. The plants float on the water's surface. Water lilies often have white or yellow flowers.

Water lilies are a source of food and shelter for animals. Beavers, fish, and some beetles eat these plants. Ducks sometimes eat water lily seeds. Water lilies also provide shelter for fish. There are 58 species of water lilies. Some species have thorns on the underside of their lily pads. These thorns protect the plant from predators such as fish.

DID YOU KNOW?
The giant water lily grows in Brazil. Its leaves are strong enough to hold the weight of a human.

White water lilies are common in North America.

There are more than 3,000 different types of dragonflies.

DRAGONFLIES

Dragonflies are long-bodied insects with four wings. Their wings allow them to hover over water and fly at fast speeds. They can fly up to 35 miles per hour (56 kmh). They can rotate their wings and fly in any direction.

Most dragonflies rely on freshwater lakes to survive. Many female dragonflies lay their eggs in water. Dragonflies can spend up to three years of their lives in the water.

Dragonflies have large, wide eyes. This allows them to see almost all their surroundings at once. They watch for predators. Birds, fish, and frogs eat dragonflies. Dragonflies also search for prey. They eat mosquitoes and other insects. Dragonflies help control insect populations. Mosquitoes and certain types of flies can spread some diseases. By eating these insects, dragonflies help reduce the spread of diseases.

ALGAE

Algae live in unmoving fresh water. They can be found in freshwater lakes and ponds. Algae live on the water's surface. They need sunlight to grow. They are often green, red, or brown. There are more than 30,000 species of algae.

Algae are an important food source for fish and other wildlife in freshwater lake ecosystems. Algae produce oxygen. Fish and other animals that live in lakes need oxygen to live. Without algae, these animals would not survive in lakes.

FRESHWATER LAKE FOOD WEB

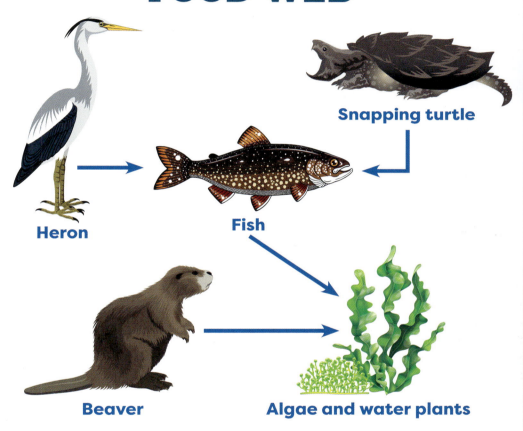

Food webs show what animals eat and how they depend on each other. If one plant or animal disappears from the food web, that affects the amount of food available for other parts of the food web.

CHAPTER THREE

Protecting Freshwater Lakes

Freshwater lake ecosystems have many plant and animal species. These living creatures need fresh water to survive. Humans rely on food sources such as fish that live in freshwater lakes. Freshwater lakes supply communities with water.

Freshwater lake ecosystems are under threat. One threat to lakes is **pollution**. A common cause of pollution is chemicals. Some farmers spray chemicals to help their crops grow. Rain carries these chemicals into lakes. Then lakes become polluted. Pollution harms and kills fish. It can also cause harmful types of algae to grow. These algae prevent other plants from growing. **Activists** are raising awareness of these threats. They educate people about the effects of pollution. They know that reducing pollution is important for the health of lake ecosystems.

People can help protect lake plants and animals by cleaning up trash in or near the water.

Ecosystem Mobile

A mobile has hanging figures or pictures. You can create a mobile to show what you have learned about freshwater lakes.

Materials
- 1 clothes hanger
- 1 piece of paper
- Colored pencils
- Tape
- 5 index cards
- Hole punch
- Scissors
- String

Directions

1. Write "Freshwater Lakes" in large letters on the piece of paper. Tape the sign to the top part of the clothes hanger.

2. Think of animals that live in freshwater lakes. Draw the animals on the index cards.

3. On each index card, write a few facts about each animal. Explain the role the animal plays in the ecosystem.

4. Use the hole punch to punch a hole in the top of each card.

5. Use the scissors to cut a piece of string. Tie one end of the string to the clothes hanger. Tie the other end to an index card.

6. Repeat for each index card until they are all tied to the hanger.

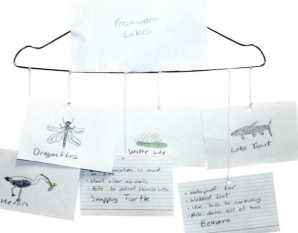

22

Glossary

activists (AK-teh-vists) Activists are people who support a cause. Activists raise awareness of threats to freshwater lakes.

ecosystem (EE-koh-siss-tuhm) An ecosystem is all of the living and nonliving things in an area. Freshwater lakes are a type of ecosystem.

pollution (puh-LOO-shun) Pollution is something harmful put in land, water, or air that makes it unclean. Pollution is a major threat to the health of lakes.

predators (PREH-duh-tuhrz) Predators are animals that hunt and eat other animals. Great blue herons and snapping turtles are predators.

prey (PRAY) Prey are animals that other animals hunt and eat. The great blue heron catches prey with its beak.

species (SPEE-sheez) A species is a specific group of living things that has the same features. Many species of plants and animals live in freshwater lake ecosystems.

Find Out More

In the Library

Kenney, Karen Latchana. *Fish Schools*. Minneapolis, MN: Jump!, 2020.

Miller, Mirella S. *Life in Freshwater Lakes*. Mankato, MN: The Child's World, 2015.

Pettiford, Rebecca. *Freshwater Food Chains*. Minneapolis, MN: Jump!, 2017.

On the Web

Visit our website for links about freshwater lakes:

childsworld.com/links

Note to Parents, Teachers, and Librarians: We routinely verify our Web links to make sure they are safe and active sites. So encourage your readers to check them out!

Index

activists, 20
algae, 18, 19, 20
beavers, 10, 11, 14, 19
dragonflies, 4, 17
food web, 13, 19
great blue heron, 4, 6, 9, 13

lake trout, 9
pollution, 20
predator, 6, 9, 13, 14, 17
prey, 6, 13, 17
snapping turtles, 13, 19
water lilies, 4, 14